Once Upon a Time, Upon a Nest

Written by
Jonathan Emmett

Illustrated by
Rebecca Harry

MACMILLAN CHILDREN'S BOOKS

Once upon a time,
upon a nest,
beside a lake,
there lived two ducks.

A mother duck

and a father duck.

There were five eggs in
the nest. Mother Duck sat
upon the nest,

all day...

and all night...

through howling
wind . . .

and driving rain,
looking after the
eggs. ALL five
of them.

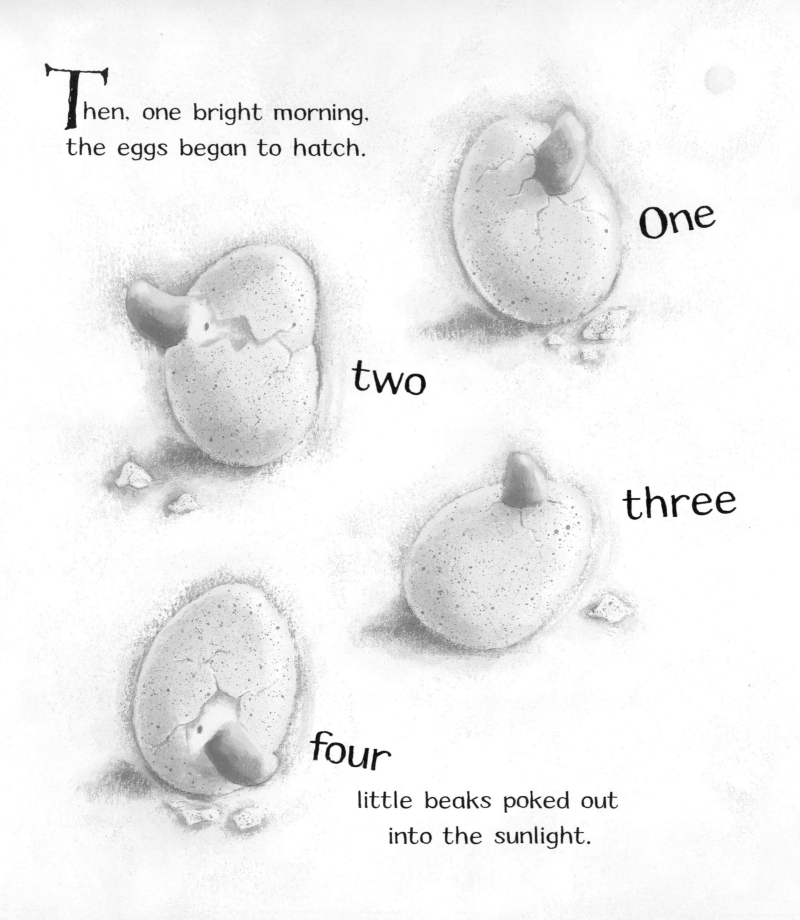

Then, one bright morning,
the eggs began to hatch.

One

two

three

four

little beaks poked out
into the sunlight.

One

two

three

four

little ducklings shook
their feathers in
the breeze.

"We'll call them
Rufus, Rory, Rosie and
Rebecca," said Father Duck.
And Mother Duck agreed.

But the fifth egg did **nothing**.

"Will it **ever** hatch?"
said Father Duck.

"It will," said
Mother Duck,
"in its own time."

And –
sure enough –

it did.

"She's very small,"
said Father Duck.
"What shall we call her?"

"We'll call her Ruby,"
said Mother Duck,
"because she's small
and precious."

Rufus, Rory, Rosie and Rebecca
ate whatever they were given.

They ate anything
and **everything**.

But Ruby ate
nothing.

"Will she
ever eat?"
said Father Duck.

"She will," said
Mother Duck,
"in her own time."

And –
sure enough –

she did.

Rufus, Rory, Rosie and Rebecca
swam off whenever they
were able.

They swam
anywhere

and
everywhere.

But Ruby swam
nowhere.

"Will she ever swim?" said Father Duck.
"She will," said Mother Duck,
"in her own time."

And – sure enough –

she did.

Rufus, Rory, Rosie
and Rebecca
grew
bigger.

And Ruby grew **bigger** too. Her feathers grew out and her wings grew broad and beautiful.

And when

and Rebecca began to fly...

Rosie

Rory

Rufus

. . . Ruby flew too!

Rufus, Rory, Rosie
and Rebecca flew far
and wide. They flew out,
across the water.
They flew up, among
the trees.

But Ruby flew farther and wider.
She flew out, **beyond** the water.

She flew up, **above** the trees.

She flew anywhere
and **everywhere.**

She stretched out her beautiful wings...

and soared high among the clouds.

Mother Duck and Father Duck
watched Ruby flying off
into the distance.

"Will she ever come back?"
said Mother Duck.
"She will," said Father Duck,
"in her own time."

And –
sure enough –

SHE DID.